Kaleidoscope 9

Kaleidoscope 9

By Debra Dickinson

Dedication

Having a book published is a dream come true, and it would not have happened without my tribe.

So, this book is dedicated to the wonderful people in my life – past and present – that lift me up, love and support me and most of all lead by example. My life is infinitely better because of you.

Thank you. I love you.

Contents

Condemned House

I found perverse pleasure as I looked at the house. The boards over the windows were rotting. I noticed the glass beneath them. "Where did the glass come from?" Growing up, it would have been nice to not always have curtains blowing through to the outside for all the world to see.

Uncomfortable with the memory, I looked at the ground and moved dirt with my shoe. I had been so proud when we first hung the curtains. We danced "Ring-around-the-Rosie," and laughed, and ran outside to see what they looked like. That was a fun day. A stupid day.

We didn't actually "hang" the curtains. Mother and I had pounded nails through them into the trim above the window. For some reason it had been okay to put holes in the trim, but not into the wall. I never understood that, but it didn't matter. We had curtains.

Now the house had glass windows and was being condemned. There was poetic justice in that. "Just goes to show that you can't escape your past." I said it out loud, directly to the house as though it were a living being, and climbed the few stairs to the porch.

The bitch mother of all condemned houses creaked and groaned with each step I took. I ignored the yellow caution tape and headed to the front door, but I stopped on the porch at the dining room window and peered through the dust and cobwebs.

It was empty now, but our dining table had been right there, in the middle of the room. Our old table was broken, and we had to stack boxes underneath it, centered just right, so the table wouldn't buckle. Dinner time was hell. I had hated them all. I wiped some more dust away from the thin glass and noticed the hole in the floor. I spoke to the house again, "Serves you right."

Then I felt bad. After all, there was a special place in the house that had saved me many times all those years ago. I sidestepped several boards that were broken or missing and entered the living room. The smell had not changed – old, wet wallpaper. The odor lingered in the air even though the wallpaper was long gone. "How is that possible?" It made me angry the house didn't answer.

Two mice scurried across the floor. They left through the same panel that had been my favorite hiding place. I didn't need to lift the panel to know what was there. More bugs, stronger stench and darkness. You'd think I'd have developed a fear of the dark, but I never did. It had been my friend. I had been safe in the dark, behind the wall, just beyond that panel. Safe there, but nowhere else.

I did a 360. Was there anything here I needed to see before they tore it down? Was there anything I would miss? Maybe, I thought. Just maybe.

I quickly but carefully walked through the kitchen to the back door. The door was gone and the screen hung on one hinge, but I could see immediately that it was still there. The old tire swing still hung from that poor tree. The steps were too shoddy to use so I jumped from the threshold to the backyard. Something about the jump made me smile, and I pulled my knife out of my pocket. Still smiling, I cut down the tire swing.

As I picked up the tire, I turned and looked at the house one last time. We had both been condemned in so many ways. I had managed to build a pretty good life for myself that was culminating in the reconstruction of this neighborhood. I was going to create a new development one house at a time, starting with this one. And God willing, there would be no foreclosures here.

I knew my architect team was not going to be happy with me.

They were going to have to spend countless hours revamping the playground because I had just decided I wanted tire swings. That meant other equipment had to be moved and load-bearing beams had to be reworked in order to meet city code and safety specifications. My last minute decision would even affect the landscape that had already been approved and ordered. Most of the team had been with me for years and they knew I rarely made such major changes just before a groundbreaking. Perhaps knowing that would soothe their pain. I smiled again as I hoisted the tire to my trunk. "Then again, probably not."

The demolition crew pulled up. I waved to them as I got in my car.

I spoke to the house one last time. "Being condemned isn't so bad. You'll come back bigger, better, stronger. Beautiful."

Freedom In Death

I stood there for a very long time, looking at him in the casket, trying to feel something. Nothing came. He looked emaciated and could have easily been one of the street bums that cities try so hard to get rid of. Joy? Was that joy that just coursed through my veins? The thought was so morbid I turned away.

I wasn't surprised to see the room sparsely occupied. It was a shame he was being buried Memorial Day weekend. It somehow implied honor and he deserved none. I took a seat in the first pew as instructed and closed my eyes. I imagined the families visiting gravesites over the weekend throughout the nation to pay homage to loved ones that did deserve such tributes. My old man had never given anything of himself his entire life, unless you counted the brutal meanness he readily bestowed on others as a gift.

It startled me when someone mistook my closed eyes for grief, and briefly laid a hand on my shoulder. She seemed like a nice, gentle, older lady, and I was wondering who she was and what she might be doing there when she spoke, "I'm so sorry for your loss dear."

I wanted to reply but had nothing to say. Then I realized I didn't have to speak. Grief stricken people aren't expected to respond, so I just gave a faint smile with a slight nod.

It all seemed so appropriate and for some reason that made me want to laugh, but I refrained. My self-imposed constraint wasn't out of respect however, especially for him. It was due mostly to fear. It occurred to me that if I started laughing, or crying, or even talking for that matter that I might never stop.

The kind lady patted my back ever so gently and moved on. I wanted to turn around to see if she sat down somewhere behind me, but I didn't want to see - not really. Seeing others meant it was

4

really happening. I was really here. The truth was that I didn't want to be seen. I just wanted to get it over with and get out of there.

Finally, someone walked up to the lectern and tapped the microphone. My brow creased. It was a priest. I didn't mind that it was a priest. I couldn't care less, but I also couldn't help but wonder if I was supposed to get someone to officiate the service.

This time I did look around. I'm not sure what I was looking for, but promptly one of the funeral attendants was at my side.

She knelt down beside me and quietly whispered, "How can I help you?"

"We're whispering?" I thought. "Really?" I looked around again, and there was no one in the pews but me and the kind lady who sat a few rows back. I realized that the other people I had witnessed earlier were staff members from the funeral home.

As if to remind me that she was still there, the young redhead said, "Miss?"

I decided to play along and whispered back, "Who is this guy?" nodding toward the priest.

"That's Father Jackson."

"Did you guys hire him?"

"We'll go over everything after the service Miss Dunley."

She left, and I once again turned to look at the little old lady sitting behind me. She nodded as if to signify understanding. My brow creased again, and I faced forward.

The priest did his thing, and I'm sure it was eloquent. I didn't listen. My mind kept going back in time to the last time I saw the bastard in the coffin. He had been arrested again, and I had gone to the jail, again. Only this time I went to tell him that I wasn't bailing him out and he would never see me again. Ever. He exploded in screams. I could still hear him ranting and raving as I walked through the lobby and left the police station. I never looked back, and he never saw me again.

I looked at the coffin now and thought about all the people that talk about angels in heaven looking down on us. I wondered if people in hell could look up. "Nah, I doubt it." I almost said it out loud and turned my attention back to the eulogy, but it was over. The priest was just finishing a prayer. I think.

He stepped off the podium and came across the aisle. He took my hand, and I stood up. As I stepped into the aisle, they were closing the casket. My back straightened and suddenly, unexpectedly I felt ten years lighter, younger.

I spoke softly as they closed the lid, "It's been years since you've seen me, and now I never have to worry about seeing you again."

The priest patted my hand and handed me a handkerchief even though I wasn't crying. I found the old-fashioned gesture touching and did not resist when he tucked my arm through his and walked with me to the foyer of the funeral home.

Once there, he gave me his card. I thought it odd that an old-fashioned priest would have a card, but then, the whole day had been odd. I took it and politely thanked him. As he walked off the little old lady approached me. I liked her. There was something about her that felt warm and safe. "How odd," I thought. "At least the day is consistent." I shook my head.

"I hope you don't mind that I hired Father Jackson. I've known him since he was a boy."

"You hired him?" I asked incredulously.

"Yes, I did."

"Who are you?"

Almost instantly, magically, another attendant was at my side and made the introduction. "Miss Elisabeth Ann Dunley, this is Liza Annette Dunley, your grandmother."

The attendant stepped away, and I stood frozen in time gaping at the woman before me. I couldn't speak, so she did, "When Jacob died…"

"Who?" I interrupted.

"Jacob," she hesitated. "Your father."

"I never called him that, and I knew him only as Jake. Please do not refer to him as a father."

She nodded in understanding once again and continued, "When Jake died, the authorities contacted me. I had not seen or heard from him in over 30 years. I did not even know I had a granddaughter until the reading of his will."

I was trying to wrap my head around it all when someone led me to a chair. Not knowing what else to do, I followed along and the little old lady, my grandmother, sat down beside me.

"He had a will?" I knew that probably should not be my first question, but it was the safest.

"Yes." And when her granddaughter looked at her with the same eyes that looked like hers 50 years before, she added, "He didn't have much as far as worldly possessions."

"Now there's a shocker." I snorted. Then added, "I'm sorry. I don't mean to be disrespectful to you."

Liza laid a gentle hand over mine on the chair arm, "It's okay," she said. "I really do understand."

The tears started flowing and as I feared, they would not stop. Liza pulled me in for a hug and I cried on her shoulder. We stayed like that for a long time.

Finally, I reached for the handkerchief Father Jackson had given me, and she pushed the hair out of my face.

"Do you have a place to stay?" she asked softly.

"No, I rode the bus here, and I haven't looked for a hotel yet."

"Then, I would like for you to come stay with me."

"I don't want to impose," and I genuinely meant that even though I wanted to be with her more than anything.

We began walking to the front door. "It's not an imposition Elisabeth. I can promise you that." I saw the limo just as the driver was opening the door.

She looked at me and winked, "My son may not have had much, but I do."

I'm not sure why, but I took a step back. I was going to decline when she turned and faced me.

"Elisabeth," she took both my hands in hers, "I have money, but I've never had a family. Your father was a fool. He had all the riches in the world because he had you. I would have given everything I own to have helped you, but I didn't know. Let me help you now."

I stood there for a moment until I knew what to say, "No, but I'll help you. How long can I stay?" I smiled a big sheepish grin and waited.

"We'll help each other child."

I climbed into the car beside her and headed to my new life. All I could think was, "I have family," and once again I laid my head on her shoulder.

Gone, But Not Forgotten

The priest was asking me to talk about it. "It helps sometimes," he said. And then he gently urged, "You were one of the few that survived the initial blast. Can you tell me about it?"

Even with my eyes closed, I could tell he was probably more curious than genuinely trying to be helpful. It didn't matter. I couldn't do anything but string together a few words anyway. They weren't even enough to form fragmented sentences, but I offered them to him in raspy breaths nonetheless.

My mind wouldn't work in complete thoughts. "Bombs everywhere. Dropping. Chaos. No visibility. Dust. Nothing normal. So much noise. Screams." I quit trying to talk and tried to swallow instead. The priest sat there a moment. Maybe he offered a prayer. Maybe he didn't. I didn't care. I never opened my eyes and finally he moved on.

I went back to sleep and the nightmares returned. They always began the same way. I'm on foot, running; to where, it doesn't matter. It was just important to get there, as fast as I could. Another bomb was about to drop. I don't know how I knew; I just did. The streets and sidewalks were no longer visible. Everything was blurred. I yelled at the driver of a Chevy S10 pickup, "Get out! Get out!"

It's a nightmare, but I'm reliving it. I'm back in that moment of time, remembering every detail.

There we were, crouched down beside his pickup. The last bomb was different, creepy. It made everything that had turned to dust seem even more eerie. It seemed to be a sonic boom followed by a bright light. The brightest I had ever seen. Then complete, utter silence. For a brief moment, the world was absolutely devoid of sound.

I looked over the cab of the truck to see the nuclear cloud several miles away. For a moment, all I could hear was my heartbeat, my labored breathing and the blood running through my veins. They were all pounding warnings into my brain. I could see the mushroom cloud but didn't want to believe it. Realization set in.

I crouched back down next to the voiceless stranger. His eyes were bigger, dilated, but nothing else about him had changed. He was motionless. He was already in shock. Poor bastard; I envied him.

I looked all around me. Some of the dust had settled. We were too far away from any other shelter. The truck was going to have to do. It wasn't much. Nothing really, and there was no way to fortify it. In a futile attempt, I braced my back against the side and poured all my strength to my thighs. I laughed, because I knew it wouldn't do any good – against the initial blast or the radiation, but I had to do something.

Then all hell broke loose.

The world blew by us, through us. There was such power in the waves of energy that passed us; it was surreal. The waves didn't take anything with them. They just consumed everything. It was power at its finest and was so forceful it almost demanded reverence. Then it was over.

I don't know why, but the first thing I did was look at my arms and hands to see if they were burned. I couldn't tell any difference, at least not initially. Then I looked at the man next to me to see if he was burned. Nothing about him had changed either. In fact, if at all possible, he seemed paler, his eyes were wider, but he was still listless, frozen in place. Then I slowly began to look around me.

The cloud that had just blown by us was stampeding the horizon, blocking my view of anything beyond it. I watched it for a moment, awestruck again at its power but already fearing its legacy. As it revealed the objects it left behind, they each look stripped, barren, lonely. It was a strange viewpoint. How could buildings look lonely?

Then I realized the cloud was leaving nothing behind that could be classified as living. There were buildings, vehicles, other structures, but no trees, no plants, no birds, and no humans. I couldn't wrap my head around the fact that we were still alive. The silence was frightening.

Movement to my left caught me by surprise. A pink, hairless dog walked up. His quivering body and bewildered eyes were asking me for help, but I didn't know what to do. He was begging for me to do something, anything, so I opened the door to the cab of the truck and let him inside. Once again I knew my actions were futile, but it was something.

There was more movement. I began to see more bewildered creatures, some human, some not. There were no birds, no vegetation, but at least there were some forms of life. I tried to convince myself that it meant something, but I knew better. I turned from the wake that the storm cloud had left behind, and looked once again over the truck to the source. I looked at the horizon and realized that it would be forever called Ground Zero, the drop zone. I was staring at oblivion.

From underneath the clouds of rolling ash and debris, I could see something oozing toward us on the ground. It was thick and glob-like, moving slowly, emitting steam or noxious gas. I couldn't tell which, but it covered most of the sloping hill and was headed in our direction.

As I scrambled to get in the bed of the truck, I started screaming at the man who had remained stationary, "Get up! You have to get off the ground. Come on!"

I pulled and clawed at him but got no response, until the strange liquid made first contact. He showed signs of life for just a moment, as if regaining consciousness, but it was too little too late. I had to let go and turn my head as the strange ooze slowly ate him, inch by inch. I prayed for my own life, not for it to be saved but that it might go quickly.

I grabbed the side of the truck as it began to sway. If it turned over, I would meet the same demise as my anonymous partner had. There was a part of me that welcomed the end, because I knew what the near future would bring. Yet another part of me still struggled for survival. Unable to choose between the two, instinct kicked in and I held on for dear life.

The truck swayed and bobbed for what seemed an eternity then settled in the cooled ooze that was no longer rolling. Everything was still, even the dog in the cab. He blinked and looked back at me through the window. For a long while, we just stared at each other.

That's where the nightmare always ends, because I honestly can't remember anything else after staring at the puppy for what seemed an eternity. I wake up in this makeshift infirmary with no idea of how I came to be here, or even where "here" is.

After realizing I am once again awake from the nightmare, I notice that everyone seems to be hurrying to get somewhere yet no one is leaving. People all around me seem to be shouting orders, yet no one is listening. I feel cold and hot all at the same time. I close my eyes again for just a moment, but now, even they hurt.

I open them again and look at the cots beside me. To my left is a stylish, elderly woman with white coiffed hair that seems to be sprouting out in all directions. Under other circumstances, she would probably be quite manicured and lovely. She smiles a faint smile as if to comfort me.

To my right is a guardsman, or marine, or is he an army man? I never could keep them straight and with most of his uniform missing, it is impossible to tell. What is unmistakable however is the alarming reality that his holster is seared to his body, as are the remaining shards of his uniform. It is horrifying to see and yet hard not to look.

Remarkably, he is able to pull his gun out of the holster and is doing so repeatedly. It is as if he is practicing for a part in a play at some western theme park. I wait for him to stop. He doesn't.

The aristocratic lady wretchedly throws up in the few inches between our cots. That catches the gunslinger's attention and he stops unholstering his gun. The sick, pretty lady struggles to get back center of her pillow.

I take advantage of the opportunity, and turn back to the gunslinger. I wait until he looks at me, and I thrust my chin in the air toward his gun. At first my vocal chords will not cooperate. They seem to be swelling by the minute, much like my skin that gives me the appearance of having been dipped in a vat of boiling lard. Finally, I speak. My voice is barely audible. I am pleased that both of them strain to hear me. That means they are interested.

I ask, "How many bullets do you have left in that thing?"

I have to repeat it when he doesn't respond, "How many bullets?"

He looks at the woman who had once been beautiful, then looks at me as if the horror is just setting in, "At least three."

I look at the pretty lady with faded blue eyes. She gives me that same faint smile once again and says, "Ladies first."

Almost in sync, as if on cue, we reach out and hold hands. I see him get the gun out of his holster one last time. I look him in the eyes with heartfelt gratitude and the lady on my left squeezes my hand as if to say the same.

There we lay, straight in our beds with chins up as if to signify pride, three nameless strangers waiting for the end that was blessedly coming sooner than later.

Coming and Going

It was hot. He was sure Texas had been hotter, but he couldn't remember when. He spat chew on the sidewalk just to see if it would sizzle; was disappointed when it didn't. Then he tried his best to blend as he stepped into the local diner.

The waitress irritated him with her birdsong, chirpy voice. He forced himself to smile before he looked up from the menu to order, "Coffee and your Cowboy Breakfast, please."

Tami found herself inexplicably edging away from him even as she poured his coffee. Determined to be friendly, she asked, "You in town for the Festival?"

"Yes, I'll be here through the Festival," he replied bluntly, curtly.

At the last booth, Agent Erin Holbrook sipped her coffee. "This is going to be fun," she thought. "Poor bastard has no clue." She was talking about Seth, the lame brain on the stool, but he was actually inconsequential to her. She was after his boss, Tommy, and had been for some time.

She had arrested Tommy many times but the charges never stuck. He had actually had the nerve to file a complaint against her after his last arrest. It was followed by a warning from the Deputy Director. That was a deterrent, but this time she knew it would be different. This time she had Tommy's youngest son, Mitch, on her side and Tommy didn't have a clue his empire was about to crumble.

Erin would never forget the day Mitch came to her office. He had walked in to the bureau building, through the lobby and straight to the admitting desk with nothing but contempt in his heart and determination on his face. It was a brazen move and Mitch did it in the middle of the day with an insolent attitude and disdain for

16

anyone that might dare report his actions to his father. He inherited the arrogance from his father, but the heart was all his.

It was unfortunate for Tommy, but a lucky break for Erin that Mitch liked his ex-stepmom, Lucy. More importantly, he loved his half brother, Michael. He was there to report that his father had put a contract out on Lucy. His father didn't know it, but Mitch had actually been the one that helped Lucy get away and relocate. He wanted Michael to have a different life, a normal life. Whatever that might be.

He was not surprised that his father had a hit ordered on Lucy with orders to bring the boy home, but he was shocked when his father had announced at dinner the night before that he had found them and was dispatching Seth. After hearing that, Mitch had spent the better part of the night making sure they were safe and secure, and had convinced Lucy to stay put until agents arrived.

As soon as she had finished taking Mitch's statement that day, Erin began organizing a sting. It was perfect and today was the day, July 4th. Erin looked at Seth again who, she noticed, somehow managed to snarl even while eating. "Enjoy your freedom you big sleazeball," she thought as she put money on the table and walked out to check on the surveillance stations.

The parade was organizing and band members tuning. It wouldn't be long.

She saw Angela setting up chairs across the street. She had convinced Lucy to let Angela, one of her best field agents, sit with the boy and pretend to be his mother. It was a wonderful coincidence that Angela looked like Lucy and was trained in profiling and hostage prevention. Things were going according to plan. Erin turned to take one last look at the goon in the diner.

He was gone. She instantly scanned the crowd, the streets, looking for Seth's height and build. Nothing.

The clowns were coming down the street with the band blaring behind them. She quickly looked at all checkpoints. Her teams were in place. Seth was nowhere to be seen. She had to break silence and alert them. At that moment a clown picked up the boy, and everyone went on alert. Just as quickly, the clown sat Michael back in his chair and ruffled his hair. As the clown got closer Erin saw it was a woman. Relieved, she realized they had dodged a bullet and she looked back at the chair. It was empty. So was Angela's. Then she saw them.

Seth had the boy. Angela was in pursuit. Erin screamed orders while on the run. She went down the side street and through the alley. She rounded the corner and barely had time to pull her gun. Soon Seth was surrounded by seven other officers. He looked at each one before concentrating on Erin.

"Let the boy go."

"I can't do that."

The flatness in his voice worried her, "Why not?"

"If I go back without him, my boss will kill me."

"Then you're in a bind because there's no way you're walking out of here with that boy."

Every agent readied their gun. He considered it for a moment and again looked from officer to officer, slowly this time. Then without warning he raised his gun and shot himself.

Later that afternoon, the agents met Lucy and her son at the airport. Michael, preoccupied with the thought of flying in a plane, seemed delighted and oblivious to the events from that morning as he talked with the pilot. His mother was apprehensive.

They were entering witness protection. While wistfully watching her son, she asked, "Will he ever see his brother again?"

Erin replied, "Mitch is a smart man. If he's also wise, I doubt it." She handed Lucy a stuffed Uncle Sam clown for Michael. "You're doing the right thing."

The two women stood for a moment and watched Michael drill the pilot with questions. Then Lucy hugged Erin and gathered her son. Erin watched as they boarded the plane and stood motionless until the plane started down the runway.

Field Agent Angela asked, "You liked them, didn't you?"

Lucy looked back at the plane, discreetly wiped her face and then turned and beamed. "Yes, yes I did. And her testimony is going to put Tommy away for a very long time."

She rubbed her hands together. "Let's go tell him. Shall we?"

Happy Birthday, Mr. President

He opened the French doors and stepped through to the veranda. It was a crisp night so he pulled his robe a little tighter. He would be taking the Oath of Office tomorrow. They had won. He had won. And it was what he wanted, wasn't it?

He leaned on the railing with both hands and hung his head. A car horn in the distance caught his attention, and he looked out over the city. Washington, D.C. never slept. "So many people," he thought. "What if I let them down?"

His wife came up behind him and wrapped her arms around his shoulders. For a moment she just laid her head on the back of his neck.

"Can't sleep?" They both knew it was a rhetorical question, but he turned to hold her and answered anyway.

"No. Not so much." He rubbed her arms and looked out over the city again. "Am I doing the right thing?"

She looked up and stared deeply into his eyes, trying to find the source of this fear that she had never witnessed before. He continued, "Our lives are never going to be the same. We knew that going into this, but if I fail, their lives are going to be worse." He pointed his chin toward the city while thinking of the nation.

She turned to shut the doors, buying time before replying. "There are some out there that would argue their lives can't get much worse. And there are those who have struggled for a long time to keep from losing more than they already have. Others have managed to keep a quality of life that they are looking to you to help them maintain. People, businesses, and this country – collectively, all need help. They've chosen you to lead the way."

He threw an arm casually over his wife's shoulder, "It's a good thing I know you're on my side or I would say 'Ouch, throw a dog a bone.' You're supposed to say something to make me feel better here."

She grinned and they braced against the wind that bit their cheeks.

He turned to take her inside.

"Just a moment," she said gently. "Let me finish... They chose the right man. You successfully ran one of the world's largest corporations for two decades. It was one of the few conglomerates in our country that didn't have to downsize or take a bailout. You took great care to keep the company's finances lean and healthy while also looking out for your employees and their financial status, as well as their personal health and well-being. I have no doubt that you will take care of We, the People of the United States of America with the same or even greater fervor." She laid a hand on his cheek and repeated with emphasis, "They chose the right man."

She looked deep into his eyes and was relieved to see some of the tension gone.

"Well, I guess that's a good thing, because it's too late to turn back now."

They both chuckled and held each other close for a long while before returning to the room.

The next day, in a world far from the likes of the presidential suite, Mary woke up a little disoriented. In a panic, she grabbed the clock and looked at the time. "Oh, thank God."

She sat the clock back down and tried to shake the cobwebs out of her head. She hated working nights but was very grateful to have found the work. It had taken her 10 months to find anything, and with any luck she'd be able to get the heat turned back on before the next cold front hit. She shivered and rubbed her arms.

She had to hurry now. The bell would ring at Kennedy's school in 30 minutes, and it was a 20-minute walk. She loved seeing him fly through the doors at the end of the day, excited about his day at school yet anxious to get home. She didn't want to miss it, so she was the one flying now.

Hand-in-hand they walked back to the apartment. She knew it wouldn't be too long before he would be too old to hold hands, but not today. Today, he was still happy to skip along beside her. She enjoyed every moment even though her feet and back hurt.

"Do you know what tomorrow is Momma?"

She knew why he was asking but decided to tease a little. "Well, I don't know about tomorrow but we get a new President today."

The frown of confusion on his face could not have been more priceless.

"By 'we', Kennedy, I mean the nation. That means you're going to have to add another name to the list when you recite the names of our Presidents."

He rolled his eyes. Impatient, he tried again. "Okay momma, but I'm talking about tomorrow. What is tomorrow?"

She laughed to herself as she answered, "Well, I'm not sure." The anguish on her son's face made her cave and she was just about to reassure him that she knew the next day was his birthday when he saw the puppy and squealed with delight.

For the life of her, she could not imagine having another mouth to feed, and could not understand why her neighbor had let her kids keep it, but Kennedy loved it too, so she released his hand

and off he ran. They spent as much time there as possible before going to their own apartment.

She was glad she had the night off, so Kennedy didn't have to spend the night next door. That meant he could wake up in his own apartment for his birthday. That, in and of itself, was a gift – for both of them.

As they got ready for bed, the neighbors across the alley were arguing again, so she turned the little black-and-white TV on. As was tradition, they put foil on their heads to match the foil on the TV antennas. It had been a game for them for as long as she could remember. She didn't want her son ever feeling sad about being poor.

The inaugural celebrations were on. Champagne flowed. Bands were playing in every city and someone was singing to the President. One announcer was talking about all the gifts that the President had received from heads-of-state all around the world.

She fought back tears and rolled her eyes as she held Kennedy a little tighter. How on earth was she going to tell her son that she didn't have a birthday gift for him? He stirred. She thought he was asleep.

"Momma, I want to be the President some day."

"That is wonderful Kennedy. Maybe you can."

"Yeah, look at all the parties and gifts he gets for his birthday!"

She looked at the screen and realized how it must appear to Kennedy.

Something shattered as the fighting escalated next door.

"Momma, if I'm President, I'm going to make everyone give you gifts too."

She kissed the top of his head. "You're a good son, Kennedy, but you need to go to sleep. You have elementary school to finish before you can think about being President."

By the time Kennedy finally crashed, they were replaying the President's acceptance speech. She didn't even bother to listen. The rhetoric had been the same every four years for as long as she could remember. She used to believe. Now she just wanted heat, a birthday gift for her son, and a raise so she could buy him a coat.

The TV station returned to the celebrations and parties. She made sure Kennedy was bundled in covers and still asleep. As she dozed off holding him tight she said, "Happy birthday, Mr. newest President. Whoop Whoop ta da ta big friggin' Whoop."

Sleeping in the Alley

She didn't mind sleeping in the alley. Not really. Especially when it was safer than staying in the house.

She was really grateful that her house was one of the homes on the block whose metal trash can stand had an extra shelf for firewood storage. The longer legs on the stand helped too. That gave her a choice. She could remove the wood logs that rested underneath the trashcans and sleep there, or it was cool enough this night that she could simply crawl underneath the stand and sleep on the ground. She had yet to make up her mind.

Susan looked up and down the alley. It was almost dark which was perfect. Some of the neighborhood kids were still playing outside, but they were down the street, on the corner, under the streetlight. It was late enough they wouldn't be coming down the alley anymore. She also made note that none of the neighbors had their back porch lights on. That meant they were probably done with yard work, grilling and all the things she had noticed other families doing outside. Still, just to be smart, she pretended she was throwing something away and removed one of the metal lids. They were all bent up which meant they got stuck sometimes. She hated when that happened, because it meant she had to wrestle to get it off the can. She didn't like touching the filthy things that much. With too much noise to suit her, she replaced the lid and looked around one more time to make sure she was alone.

She heard something shatter inside the house and could hear the yelling that was muffled from this distance. She had snuck out just in time.

She decided she was too tired to mess with taking the logs off the stand. Besides, she didn't want to take a chance that she might forget to put them back. She did forget one time and her stepfather had a fit. He interrogated her for hours wanting to know if she knew which one of the neighborhood hooligans had done it. She was terrified that he was going to figure out that not only had she been the one to remove the logs, but why. He never did.

As she crawled under the trash can stand, she mumbled out loud, "That's because you're so stupid!" She stuck her tongue out in the direction of the house and was about to curl up when she heard it.

She froze in place. She slowed her breath so she could hear better. Wide-eyed, she waited. He got closer, but already she knew it was her friend, Lee. She wanted to chuckle but didn't dare because it would give her hiding place away. Lee was so proud of the new bike he got for his birthday. No one had the heart to tell him that it squeaked and rattled so loudly that you could hear it for blocks away. She smiled and watched him fly by.

He was probably headed home for dinner. Lee never missed a meal. This time she did chuckle. No one had the heart to tell him too that his bike was half the size he needed. She liked her friends. Most of them were kind.

She caught her breath again, however, when he hit the brakes and did a fishtail to start heading back toward her.

He stopped right in front of her and asked, "Susan, what are you doing down there?"

"Shhhh!" Horrified, she waved him to go on as she barely peeked out from under the stand.

"Seriously," he added. "What are you doing down there?" He dropped his bike and knelt down in the grass beside her. "Is it a snake?"

"A snake?" She crawled quickly out from under the trashcans and looked wildly behind her in a panic before she realized he simply did not understand.

Something else broke in the house and her mother screamed. This time it wasn't so muffled.

"Geez," Lee said, and stared at the house.

"Go home, Lee. Don't you need to eat or something?" Her voice was unkind and she felt ashamed.

He looked at her and could tell she was embarrassed. "What are you going to eat?"

Susan had not thought about it. Until now. "Great," she thought. "Now I'm going to be hungry all night." She rolled her eyes.

"Wait here. I'll be right back." He hopped on his bike and sped off before she could say anything.

She didn't want him to come back. Traffic around her hiding place was not what she needed. Suddenly the back door to her house flew open and she frantically crawled back under the bin.

"Susan!" her stepdad yelled. "SUUUSAN!" He repeated her name several times.

It was routine, and she knew he'd give up. She knew too it would make him angry that she wasn't there, and she also knew that he would take it out on her mother. "God forgive me," Susan thought. She couldn't help but feel grateful that it wasn't her getting the beating.

She wasn't sure how much time passed because she had dozed off. She didn't even hear Lee walk up. He shook her shoulder and whispered, "Susan. Hey, I brought you something."

The night sky was pitch-black. She quickly glanced back at her house. All the lights were off. A little disoriented, she crawled out from under the bin and sat on the ground next to Lee. "Where's your bike?" she whispered back.

"I parked it down at the end of the alley. That thing doesn't have a quiet part on it."

They both giggled with their hands over their mouth.

He held out a dishtowel. "You brought me a towel?" Susan asked.

"No, silly." Lee said. "I brought you food."

All she could do was stare. And blink.

"Don't you like it?" Lee asked.

"Yes." Susan replied softly. "Very much."

It was the nicest, kindest thing anyone had ever done for her. And, it was the best pork chop and homemade biscuit she had ever had. Her mom didn't cook much. She glanced nervously back at the house.

To distract her, Lee said, "I brought you something else." He reached underneath his jacket.

"Uh, I guess this is just a towel." This time it was his turn to be embarrassed.

Susan quickly thanked him and took it from him. She had no idea why he brought her a towel, or why it meant so much to her, but it did. She unfolded it. It was a large beach towel. She hugged it close to her and smiled.

Her response made Lee beam with pride. "I thought you could lie down on it. Beats the wet grass."

With that she gave him a quick kiss on the cheek, and this time they both looked embarrassed.

After a minute, Lee asked, "Can I ask you something?"

With a shrug of her shoulders Susan said, "Sure."

"Do you sleep out here very often?"

With another shrug of her shoulders Susan replied, "Sometimes."

She knew that wasn't really a full answer to the question he was really asking, but it was the best she had to give.

He sat there a moment longer and hesitantly said as he stood up, "Well, I better be getting back."

She waited until he finished brushing off his jeans, "Lee?"

He looked at her, "Yeah?

"Thank you." He started to shrug it off. She quickly said, "No, Lee," and waited until he looked at her again. "Thank you."

He sheepishly grinned, and simply said, "You're welcome."

As he walked off, she had no way of knowing they were forging a friendship that would last a lifetime. All she knew was that she slept better in the alley that night than she had slept anywhere her entire life.

Return to Sender

She took the envelope out of the mailbox and stared at it for a very long time. A red felt tip marker had been used to write the words in big, bold letters, "Return to Sender."

Exclamation marks and underlines had been added for emphasis. It didn't surprise her that he had returned the sympathy card unopened. In fact, looking at it now, the only thing that surprised her was that he had not used real blood to send it back.

So if she wasn't surprised, why did she find herself suddenly sitting on the curb, still clutching and staring at the envelope?

She sat there for quite a while, frozen in time. She thought about getting up several times but couldn't make her muscles move. After all these years, why was he still so damn important to her?

She was 23 when they had married. For most people, that would be a good age to marry. Not for her. It had taken her another 15 years to mature, but by then it was too late. The marriage had "irreconcilable differences." Sitting on the curb, she hung her head in shame.

A neighbor drove by and honked. It was enough to stir her and pull her out of the gutter – almost literally and figuratively.

She stood up and shut the door to the mailbox without gathering the rest of the mail. The walk from the street to her front door and through to the kitchen seemed like miles. She carefully laid the envelope down and called her best friend. They had met at a Crafters Camp two decades before and had been friends ever since. There was an age difference, but it had never mattered.

"Britt?" she asked, and wondered why people bother with such rituals as asking someone's name when you obviously know who it is.

Britt didn't answer but simply asked her own question, "What's wrong Marj?"

Marjorie smiled. Yes, her friend knew her best.

"He returned the envelope unopened. Looks like you were right. Mind if we change the bet from money to a Margarita? I'll gladly buy."

"Sure. Let me check with Bry to see if he can get Jakey to practice. I'll call you back in just a few."

Marjorie hung up and thought about the nicknames they all had for each other. She was Marj. Brittany was Britt. Bryan was Bry and poor Jake, their son, was Jakey. It had been cute when he was little, but as a young man it hadn't always sat so well with him. She smiled, because she knew no matter how much he protested, he would always be Jakey.

The phone rang. "I'll pick you up in 10."

Marjorie went back out to the curb and once again sat down. She had the fleeting thought that the curb was where she belonged, and then dismissed it. She had come a long way in pulling her life together. She wasn't going to let a damn envelope with his scribbles on it negate everything.

Britt pulled up and she climbed in.

"O'Hara's?"

"That's fine."

They rode in silence the entire way.

The host greeted them. "Hello Mrs. Waverly, Ms. Sterling. Would you like a booth or a table this --?"

Marjorie interrupted, "A table please, Walt." And she added as an afterthought, "On the patio. Lakeside."

Britt did nothing more than take notice of her friend's mood as she fell in step behind Walt and Marjorie.

Walt showed them to their table, reviewed the daily specials and told them Katie would be their server for the evening.

Marjorie gave the impression that she was giving her menu thorough attention. Brittany wasn't buying any of it.

"So, the next thing I know, you'll be ordering a round of shots for us, the rest of the people on the patio, and the patrons inside. You will party like you're the happiest girl on earth and act like nothing is wrong. Is that how tonight is going to go?"

Marjorie lowered her menu and with attitude and icy eyes, turned on her friend, "That's not fair Britt, and you know it."

"Yes. I know it. But, I stand by it. Where are you going with this Marj? Are you here to just drink and eat and not talk? If so, I've got a family I need to get back to."

Marjorie studied her friend for a moment and then caved, "He didn't even read it Britt. All that time and effort, and he didn't even read it."

"The man lost his wife just a few months ago, sweetheart. Give him a break."

The server, who was over the top and way too bubbly to suit Marjorie, approached the table and began reciting the specials again. To spare her life, Britt interrupted and said, "Two margaritas please."

Marj added, "Large."

"No." Britt quickly corrected. "Make that two SMALL margaritas." She kept her eyes on her friend for effect.

Waitress 101 hadn't told Katie, the restaurant's newest server, what to do in situations like this, so she just stood there. Britt patted her hand without taking her eyes off Marj, and repeated, "Two small margaritas Katie. Now run along dear."

Marjorie waited until the waif was out of earshot and then snapped at her friend, "That was mean. To both of us."

"All I know is that he returned your card unopened. You're giving me facts, but not really talking. Start talking and I'll stay here all night with you if that's what you want. But you're not going to just drown your sorrows and bury your feelings and tell me the obvious. I know he returned the card. What I want to know is why that is bothering you so."

Someone brought them some water and Marjorie played with the straw. "Did I ever tell you what I finally decided to write in the card?"

"No. You didn't. And Marj?" Britt waited until her friend looked at her. "I'm sorry he hurt you – yet again."

Marjorie shrugged. "I had it coming." She paused and added with a shrug, "Yet again." Before her friend could protest, she continued, "I did Britt. No matter how much I wish that weren't true, we both know it is."

She went back to playing with her straw again and quoted from memory what she had written:

I was a horrible wife and put you through hell. I will always regret that. In time, I became very grateful that you found happiness and love with Gina. I recently learned of her passing, and I am so sorry for your loss. I hope the time you had, and the memories you shared, are of comfort. You deserve all the best life has to offer, and I hope this finds you doing well. Take care of yourself. Blessings!

Sincerely,

Marj

The drinks arrived and both ladies took a sip and looked out over the lake for a moment.

Britt broke the silence. "What did you want to happen Marj?" Her friend looked puzzled, so she repeated, "When you sent the card Marj, what did you want to happen?"

Marjorie thought about it before answering, "Mostly I just wanted to convey my condolence, but I suppose, on some level, I want his forgiveness. And his acceptance. He clearly still thinks I'm this big 3-headed Medusa aberration cross-bred with Linda Blair from The Exorcist."

Katie walked up to take their order, so Britt took advantage of the opportunity and asked her, "Katie, do you know who Linda Blair is?"

The young girl shook her head side-to-side and stared blankly at the two women.

"How about The Exorcist? Do you know that movie, the original, not the remake or sequels?"

Again, Katie shook her head.

Brittany let her off the hook, "We're not ready to order. Can you come back in about 10 minutes?"

Katie gratefully scurried off.

Both women chuckled lightly. Then Brittany took Marjorie's hands and held tight. "Marj, even your analogy of what you think he thinks of you is stuck in the past. You have got to let it go. You have got to let him go."

Marjorie hung her head just as she had earlier, "Over the years, of all the ways I pictured them breaking up, not a single one of those scenarios included Gina dying. What a rotten deal. My heart truly breaks for him Britt."

"I know it does."

"I used to have this fantasy that they would split up and we'd run into each other somewhere, and he would see how well I'm doing. Once and for all he would know I'm not this scary, evil person. I don't know why his acceptance is so important to me, but I worked hard day in and day out to become someone he'd be proud of. Now it doesn't even matter."

Brittany tried to wrap her head around that and sat back with her drink for a moment.

Then she leaned forward and looked her friend directly in the eyes, "You mean to tell me that you built your career, your world, around the hope that you would get him back one day?"

Hearing it said out loud, by someone else, even if that someone else was Brittany, made Marjorie feel ridiculous.

"I did it for me too. Even if we never got back together, I wanted to be someone that he would like. I had something to prove – to him, and to me. Then in the end, all I wanted him to know was that I was sorry. I was sorry for the horrible wife I had been, and sorry that he had lost Gina after all these years. That's such a crappy break."

"How many years were they married?"

Marjorie looked at Brittany in disbelief. She couldn't figure out what her friend was up to. Brittany had been with her at the courthouse for the divorce, and she knew full well that he had married Gina just 3 months after that. She already knew the answer.

"Why do you ask?"

"Just answer me Marj. How long were they married?"

"Seventeen years."

"Seventeen years and you're still grieving. Now you're including his loss of Gina in that grief. You have got to let him go."

"He still thinks I'm a horrible person and a loser. That's the part I don't know how to let go."

"Oh, I know what to do then. You should send him another card."

With eyes wide and mouth open, Marjorie looked at Brittany as though she had lost her mind.

The look on Marj's face made Brittany laugh. Katie walked up to the table again and before Brittany could get her composure, Marjorie ordered the next round, "Two LARGE margaritas Katie." Before Britt could protest, Marj quickly, literally shooed Katie away.

"Now who's being mean?" Brittany asked, wiping the tears of laughter from her eyes.

Determined, Marj pounced, "Okay, spill it Britt. Why on earth do you think I should send him another card?"

"Oh, this is such a great idea I actually think you should have the card blown up to life size. Better yet, you can hire a quartet to deliver it as a sing-o-gram!"

Frustrated, Marjorie sat back in her chair, "Okay, now you really have lost it. I should have asked for the ticket instead of two more drinks."

With her eyes twinkling and tongue in cheek, Brittany defiantly said, "Send him something with this message: You can visit my past if you want to, but I don't live there anymore."

The words touched Marjorie to the core of her soul.

Brittany continued, softly, "He returned that card to someone he used to know, Marj. He doesn't know you. The real you. The you that you have worked so hard to become. Let him go girl."

Marjorie looked up at her with water-filled eyes, and Brittany softly repeated, "Let him go."

Oblivious to the moment, Katie walked up with their drinks and a request, "Miss Dixon?"

Marjorie was surprised that the waitress called her by her pen name, "Yes?"

Katie took the book off her tray and continued, "The ladies at that table on the rail want to know if you will sign their book."

Marjorie wiped the tears from her eyes and took the pen from Katie. "Did they give you their names?"

"Yes ma'am." Katie handed her a slip of paper with the ladies' names on it and Marjorie scribbled something. She gave the ladies a nod and a smile as she handed the book and the pen back to Katie.

"Katie?"

"Yes ma'am."

"Their bill is on me."

"Yes ma'am."

She smiled at her friend. "I really don't live back there anymore, do I?"

Once again her friend reached across the table and held her hands, "No. You live right here, right now. You have a beautiful life and you are a beautiful person. It is his loss to not know that."

Marj hung her head for just a moment, and then looked out over the water again, "I loved him, you know? I should never have lost him, but I hadn't faced my demons yet. We ran out of time."

Brittany nonchalantly picked up her menu, snapped it open and said, "Sounds like a good book to me, Marj." She gave her friend a wink.

Marj looked at her and thought about it for a moment. The muse struck and her writing gears began spinning. With her spirits lifted, Marj replied, "Yes. Yes, it does, doesn't it? Let's order. I'm starved."

With a big smile they both waived for Katie.

The Blue Lady

They weren't threatening. They weren't even aware of their surroundings. They certainly weren't aware of me, but I couldn't take my eyes off of them. I had to move out of the way or be trampled by the people hurrying to finish their shopping and get home. But still, I could not divert my attention. Didn't anyone else notice? Why was I the only one mesmerized?

I couldn't enter the store. Not just yet. They stopped me dead in my tracks as they came through the exit side. Years later I would be able to articulate that moment in time, but for a long time, and certainly at that time, it was an inexplicable freeze frame of life.

I managed to find a bench at the corner of the store that gave me a perfect view of them loading their car. I sat down and prayed that no employees would come out to take their smoke break anytime soon. The overflowing, stale ashtray was dirty and filthy enough, but it seemed even more vulgar in direct contrast to the two ladies I chose to watch. They were pristine, almost flawless. I wondered if the older lady smelled of lilac or baby powder. It would have been fitting. Why were they so fascinating? Blue. That's all I could think. Both of them, everything about them, blue.

The hair on the little old lady was even blue with a touch of silver that seemed to dance on her head. Her eyes were blue, vibrant blue like the Caribbean. I bet she was a looker in her younger days. Her crisp two-piece suit was royal blue and she donned a matching pill hat, the small boxy kind you only see in the movies. And even though we're in the 21st century, I almost expected her to have crisp, white gloves to match. She didn't, but she did have the navy blue patent purse, complete with a silver clasp and a short leather band braced sturdily over her forearm. Her shoes matched exactly and the patent leather shone like moonlight on a lake.

What were they doing here? Not only at this wretched, giant superstore, but here, in this century? I glanced around. Still no one else seemed to notice. They walked up to the 1st car in the row, a handicapped space. I couldn't make out the model, but the car had to be every bit as old as the lady with the royal blue pill hat. The car was huge. The steering wheel reminded me of a captain's wheel on a yacht. And yes, the car was blue. Three different shades of blue, in fact. Of course it was. I spared a grin.

They had done this before, the two of them, together – probably many, many times. I realized the other one was a nurse. Her dark blue, almost black uniform indicated such. She was much younger than the other, but still no spring chick, as my dad would have said. She was pushing the cart, and the blue-haired lady walked arm-in-arm with her. As they approached the car, the nurse in dark blue braced the cart and walked to unlock the door. They never spoke, but each knew what the other was going to do. As the nurse unlocked the car, the little old lady waited at the cart patiently. Looking around, and finally looking up at all the nasty grackles gathered in the scrawny trees of the littered median.

"You belong on an estate with beautiful trees and songbirds," I almost said out loud. Wishing somehow I could make it come true for her. She was so out of place. For a moment, she looked lost.

The nurse returned and held out her arm. Arm-in-arm once again, she walked the little old blue lady to the back seat where she slid in. Still they never talked. They never really even looked at each other. The nurse didn't shut the door. That surprised me. Instead, she went around to the right front passenger door and got something out of the glove box. "Glove box," I thought to myself. "Now that's funny."

She came back quickly and leaned in to the little old blue lady. I realized concern was building for two people I didn't even know.

Did she have to get something medicinal? Was the little old blue lady okay? Then the nurse stood up and walked to the back of the car to start unloading the cart, and I got a glimpse of the little old blue lady again. She was smoking. The nurse had gathered a cigarette and lit it for her. She was smoking and you guessed it, exhaling puffs of blue.

I was trying to absorb the images, make sense of it all, and somehow wrap my brain around this duo that didn't belong. They didn't seemingly belong together in this day and age, and certainly they didn't belong in that parking lot, in that neighborhood.

The nurse in dark blue shut the trunk and delivered the cart to its holding pen. As she came around the tri-blue car, she pulled the cigarettes out of her uniform pocket and leaned in to light yet another for the little old blue lady. This time she also fastened her seat belt. As was clearly their pattern, they never spoke or looked at one another. The entire car was almost filled with pillows of blue smoke. The little old blue lady was enjoying every puff.

I became very conscious that I was staring. I had been so fascinated to this point that it had not even occurred to me that I was borderline voyeur, far more than just rude. Still, I didn't want to stop. I made myself look away for just a moment. Only to look back and catch them laughing.

They were both bent forward in their seats. The nurse in the dark blue uniform was grasping the steering wheel and bent over laughing. The little old blue lady was leaning forward and holding her pill hat with her cigarette still poised between her fingers. She was also laughing hysterically.

The nurse had pulled out of the parking space and tried to turn the giant yacht of a car the wrong way. She had quite literally put herself between a rock and a hard place. Almost just as quickly as they had started laughing, they stopped, and gathered themselves. The nurse turned completely around in her seat to make sure her precious cargo was okay. It was so strange to see them talk. There was a gentle love between them, not just routine after all. The little old blue lady waved her hand around in the cloud of blue smoke to indicate she was okay and the nurse pulled the tri-blue giant car forward, back into the original parking space.

I looked around. Did anyone see that? Yes, several had. Now many were staring. Standing in place actually, gawking. Finally, I didn't feel so strange for finding them so hypnotic. I felt vindicated.

As they backed out of their space again, this time headed in the right direction, the little old blue lady finished positioning her royal blue pill hat, and the nurse in dark blue uniform positioned the mirror of the tri-colored blue boat. They were back to silent mode, chins up and off to wherever they had come from. Could it have been a time machine? I almost wished for them that it were. I got up from my seat just as smokers came out to take their break.

One of them had a nose ring, the other a Mohawk and the girl was smacking gum while adjusting her bra that was showing. I looked to the top of the parking lot. The little old blue lady must have rolled down her window because blue smoke billowed out. One of the kids asked the other for a light. Despicable profanity was exchanged, and I found myself sorely missing my two blue friends that had just left.

I headed straight to the women's department and bought myself a blue outfit. Since I wasn't about to take up smoking, and probably wouldn't find a working time machine, it would have to do. I never saw them again, but to do this day, blue is my favorite color. All shades.

A Sense of Wonder

She was so excited to see him. It had been several years. They had a fling once, but over time they had settled into an affectionate friendship. They kept in touch by phone or email, but she had not seen him since her diagnosis. She wondered if she could still hold her own.

She loved the way his mind worked, and in the past they enjoyed stimulating conversations. Owen was a brilliant artist entrenched as a successful playwright in the New York community, and she was a former biologist turned romance novelist. Boondocking was the thread that held them together. Now she no longer lived in an RV and couldn't even drive.

She watched him pull into the driveway and could barely wait for him to get out before she had him wrapped in a giant bear hug. Nothing else mattered except that he had driven across three states to see her while she still knew his name, while she could still talk, while she still could appreciate his fab van.

She took a step back and whistled. "Look at you," she said, talking to the van and not her friend. Then she turned to him and said, "I am so proud of you. Look at what you built."

They didn't even exchange the normal niceties. He unlocked the side door, and she climbed in to marvel at his handiwork. She was quite certain he was the only millionaire traveling the U.S. in his built-by-hand classic Vanagon. She loved it! And she realized, she loved him – not the gooey romantic love she had once hoped for, but the comfortable kind that fits like a favorite pair of slippers or favorite t-shirt. She gave him another hug.

They would only be together for a couple of days before he caught a flight and headed east to see his dad. She didn't want to miss a minute, and they settled into patio chairs to start swapping stories.

Only it wasn't long before she realized she wasn't as quick as she used to be, and what he was mistaking for errors in wording, or gaps in storyline, was actually the result of her traumatic brain injury, commonly referred to as a TBI. She allowed the corrections without reminding him the reason. For once, just for 48 hours, she didn't want to be someone with a TBI or possibly even dementia that the doctors were beginning to suspect. She just wanted to be able to have an animated dialogue with her friend. She missed being able to connect with him like they used to. By night's end, it hadn't happened.

She couldn't help but wonder if he had noticed, or had he just thought she was incoherent, magically dropping 20 IQ points since their last visit? It was frustrating – not just that he seemed to think her incongruence in conversation was normal, but that she had no way of explaining any of it to him. It was her first realization that the art of conversation was getting lost along with everything else. She closed her eyes and prayed that he would sleep well in his van, and that she would not have a seizure during the night.

When she opened her eyes the next morning, she immediately gave praise for having clarity of mind. She almost laughed – clarity of mind was subjective. These days, for her, it meant she knew where she was, what she had done the day before and for the most part, what she hoped to do during the present day. Carrying that out was often an entirely different story.

She was grateful when her friend invited her to go with him to run errands. She was going to get to GO. Her reaction reminded her of her furbabies. Mention the word "go" to them and they bounce up and down, run in circles, talk, pant and lead the way to the car. She forced herself to follow her friend instead of leading, and chuckled at the thought of panting. When he couldn't see, as he walked around to the driver's side, she quickly clapped her hands and smiled ear-to-ear. He opened the door and they were off.

She didn't care where. He told her, but she already forgot. She was happy to just tag along, and was glad her silence didn't seem unusual to him. In fact, she knew that he actually preferred it. On occasion though, she couldn't contain her excitement. There were so many new sights, sounds, and smells. She realized she had probably gone overboard when she stuck her head out the window to feel the crisp air. While enjoying the sensation of her hair blowing, she laughed and cheerily cried, "wind in the hair," only to see confusion on her friend's face when she was done. She hesitated, but decided to roll up her window to avoid any further temptation.

They continued down the road and she was amazed it had so many curves. As they rounded each one, she couldn't wait to see what was around the bend, and even though they were in the city, there were lots of trees and undeveloped acreage on each side of the road. She exclaimed with a huge smile, "Isn't this a wonderful road?"

Her friend replied, "It's just a road."

She wanted to explain what she had seen and felt, but the words just weren't there. So she asked him a question, "Don't you see? It isn't just a road. No roads are. Because they lead to somewhere. That makes each one of them special." She waited; proud of the explanation she had formed.

"That's a road by definition."

She couldn't argue with that, but she couldn't process it either so she returned to her silence. She decided she would love the road enough for everyone – all roads, in fact. And her silent prayer was that she would one day be able to travel down them once again on her own. Then, she could take all the time she wanted to discover what was just beyond each bend.

She was deep in thought when they pulled into the grocery store. It was a mega supermarket plus store. She had not been inside one, but had wanted to see this one since moving to the area. As they walked down the parking lot toward the front door, she thought of the lane in which they were walking as another road. In awe, she looked up at the huge store and thought, "Wow, road. Look what you lead to."

When they got inside, the activity was overwhelming. She thought about retreating to the car, but her friend was already at the ATM. She stood in place and just watched ALL of the people. She became enthralled with each one. There were patient ones, the ones in a hurry, slow ones, talkative ones, sad ones, happy ones, ones with family, and ones without. SO many people!

And the store itself was lovely. Everything was color coordinated and all of the displays were stunning. There were lights everywhere – small, twinkly lights like Christmas, and there were even chandeliers over some of the displays. At the end of each aisle there were old-fashioned train lights. She had never experienced a store like this before. Or, at least she no longer remembered if she had. It was a new experience for her, and she loved every minute of it.

Owen was off again. She had to hurry to catch up with him. "Where are we going?" she asked.

"I want to get an avocado to go with the hamburgers tonight. What do you want?"

She thought about it for a moment and replied, "A tomato."

He frowned, and she tried to remember if a tomato goes on a hamburger. She was quite certain it did so his frown confused her.

"We should have gone to a farmer's market. You're not going to find a good tomato here."

"Why not," she asked.

She looked around at all of the pretty displays while they walked by more items she had never seen before. She couldn't imagine anything in this store not being good. She wished she could have more time on her outing to just walk around and gawk.

Her friend was talking. He was saying something about nutritional value, New Jersey tomatoes, California tomatoes, and smell.

"Smell?" she asked as they rounded the corner to the produce section.

She stopped dead in her tracks and her mouth flew open. She had never seen so many tomatoes in her life.

"What's wrong?" Owen asked.

"There are so many tomatoes," she exclaimed.

There was a whole wall of them. There was quite possibly more produce in this one place than she had seen in her whole life. Once again, the whole experience was so overwhelming that she thought about retreating to the safety of the van. Only by now, she was completely lost. And staring at a wall of tomatoes.

"Good luck on finding a good one," her friend said, and continued, "Even if you find one that has a good aroma, it's probably not going to be that tasty."

She began picking up tomatoes and smelling them. She found a few that smelled very strong.

"Owen, are these good?"

He replied, "That's the vine you smell, not the tomato."

So she decided to smell only the ones without vines. After a while Owen laughed and asked, "Are you going to smell every one of them?"

She picked out the very next one that had any smell to it at all, noting that she hadn't even made it halfway down the wall of tomatoes. She wondered, "What do people do with all of these tomatoes?"

Her friend walked up to the baskets of avocados and began rummaging through them. She kept watching the people and lights. Eventually he handed her one, "Here, what do you think of this one?"

She smelled it. He grinned, "You don't smell avocados."

She handed it back to him and tried very hard to remember what was supposed to be done to pick out an avocado. She couldn't actually remember ever having bought one. Surely she had. She tried harder to remember. Owen was walking off.

"I want some ice cream for tonight," he announced and then asked, "What kind do you like?"

She was trying to remember. The last few times her friend Judy had taken her to the grocery store, she had bought vanilla. She tried harder to remember what other kinds she liked, but got distracted.

So many people. She saw the man that had come into the store while her friend was at the ATM. The man had been upset because there weren't any more baskets. It confused her, because there were a lot of baskets right in front of him. He grumbled about having to go to the other side of the store to get one. She had almost stopped him to point out all of the baskets, but he hurried off too quickly. Now she was glad she had not done that because it was a small hand-carry basket he had wanted. He seemed happy now that he had one. She decided to talk to him.

"I see you found a basket," she said gleefully.

The man startled and looked confused, even a little scared.

She pointed to the basket, "I was at the front of the store when you couldn't find one. I'm glad you have one now."

"Oh," he said in recognition. "Yes, it was frustrating, but they had some on the other side."

"Well, I'm happy you got one." She was going to reach out and pat him on the arm because it had been so distressing for him, but he had that scared look again, so she decided to leave him alone.

She followed her friend to find ice cream. While walking, he asked her where the frozen section was. She was trying to remember what she buys in the frozen section and was proud to remember that she buys pizza there. "But he's not after pizza," she thought, and so she answered, "I don't know. I've never been here before."

He made a few turns and exclaimed that he could see it. He started walking faster and all of the twists and turns and noise were confusing her. He stopped. She ran into him. And even though she was mortified, she couldn't help but laugh. So did he.

"What happened to all that talk we had earlier about respecting space?" he joked.

They both kept laughing, and she followed him to the ice cream, trying very hard not to stay right behind him. But it was scary to allow too much distance - she didn't want to get lost.

They walked up to the glass doors and her friend made another announcement. "I think I'm going to get coffee ice cream."

"Coffee ice cream!" she exclaimed. She had no idea they made coffee ice cream! Then she realized that he might be kidding her so she asked, "Really? They make coffee ice cream?"

He wasn't quite sure whether or not she was serious, but he replied, "Um, yeah. It's one of the top 10 flavors in the USA."

Now she knew he was joking, "No it's not."

He pulled out a carton of coffee ice cream. Her eyes got big. He was walking again, and the whole space thing was really hard to figure out since she was still trying to wrap her mind around coffee ice cream.

He asked her if she was serious that she had never had it. She answered, "I didn't even know they made it."

It was difficult to talk and think about coffee ice cream and stay close, but not too close, and not get lost. She concentrated harder, and was grateful when they got to the checkout stand.

She asked the cashier, "Did you know they make coffee ice cream?"

The cashier had her own favorite, but it was not the same as her friend's. Owen and the cashier had a lively discussion about it. She couldn't follow any of the finer points they were making about coffee ice cream, so she nodded and smiled. She couldn't wait to get home and try coffee ice cream.

They were walking again.

The parking lot was busier than the store. Cars were zipping by – people were crossing and zigzagging in all directions. She stood there and realized her friend was already across the road. She waited a moment and decided to risk it. She barreled across the road as bravely as her friend and ran into a man, almost tripped on a baby stroller being pushed by a woman in a hurry, and barely dodged a grocery cart that was apparently in a race for the front door. She quickly ran to her friend and grabbed his arm. That felt uncomfortable, but at least she had the space thing down now.

It was surreal to realize that not only could she no longer do things by herself, but apparently she needed a Seeing Eye dog of sorts. But, in this moment she was deliriously happy and nothing else mattered. Tonight she was going to have hamburgers with tomato and avocado, coffee ice cream for dessert, and visit with her friend before he left for the airport to go see his dad. As she got back in the van, she decided to roll the window down and hang her head out all the way home.

About Debra Dickinson

Debra believes in Oneness and the infinite connection that flows through all existence as Universal Spiritual Energy, known by many names. She shares her personal knowing, "All that has ever been, all that will ever be, already exists. It is our awareness that expands."

She has three favorite quotes:

"I didn't change, I just woke up."

- Author unknown

"I fairly sizzle with zeal and enthusiasm and spring forth to do that which should be done by me."

- Charles Fillmore

"God constantly speaks to us through each other as well as from within."

- Father Thomas Keating

She holds strongly that we are spiritual beings having a human experience and that God can use infinite vessels and portals to reach our hearts. She finds it ironic that her first book to be published has no mention of spirituality. She writes what flows. She lives from her heart.

And she's had many lives. She was the first in her family to graduate high school and attend college, graduating with a degree in Biology from the University of North Texas in Denton with honors. In the past, she's held a real estate license, was a master Scuba instructor, drove her own Harley, and enjoyed parasailing and repelling. Outdoor activities soothe her soul. She enjoys walks with her two dogs and stargazing, and loves living in her van.

She survived childhood abuse, domestic violence in her first marriage, overcame alcohol addiction and has made peace with having multiple marriages and no children. She has had countless jobs in a myriad of fields – a career kaleidoscope. No longer able to work full-time due to a traumatic brain injury, she says, "Any day above ground not drooling, is a good day." She vows to never lose her sense of humor. Although she requires quiet and solitude to process, she is grateful for an illness that mandates living in the moment. Her biggest hope is that she never loses her God-given talent for writing. She has many books, in many different genres, waiting their turn to be published.

To learn more about Debra, visit her website at debradickinson.com